A King filled
a room with cheese.

Yum, yum!

A mouse sniffed the cheese.

It crept out and
began to munch.

Soon, hundreds were munching the cheese.

The King got lots of cats to get rid of them.

Next, the King got lots of dogs to get rid of the cats.

Then, the King needed to get rid of the dogs...

“I need a mouse,” wailed the King. “In fact, I need lots of them!”

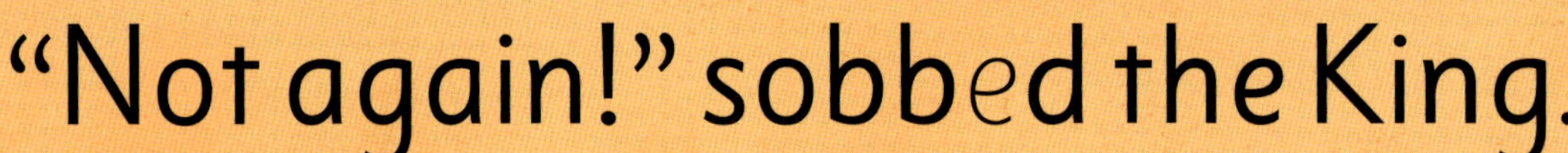

Will I ever get the cheese?